MISSION
CATASTROPHE

Stories From Kent

Edited By Brixie Payne

First published in Great Britain in 2019 by:

 Young**Writers**®
Est. 1991

Young Writers
Remus House
Coltsfoot Drive
Peterborough
PE2 9BF
Telephone: 01733 890066
Website: www.youngwriters.co.uk

FOREWORD

Young Writers was created in 1991 with the express purpose of promoting and encouraging creative writing. Each competition we create is tailored to the relevant age group, hopefully giving each student the inspiration and incentive to create their own piece of work, whether it's a poem or a short story. We truly believe that seeing their work in print gives students a sense of achievement and pride in their work and themselves.

Our Survival Sagas series, starting with Mission Catastrophe and followed by Mission Contamination and Mission Chaos, aimed to challenge both the young writers' creativity and their survival skills! One of the biggest challenges, aside from facing floods, avoiding avalanches and enduring epic earthquakes, was to create a story with a beginning, middle and end in just 100 words!

Inspired by the theme of catastrophe, their mission was to craft tales of destruction and redemption, new beginnings and struggles of survival against the odds. As you will discover, these students rose to the challenge magnificently and we can declare *Mission Catastrophe* a success.

The mini sagas in this collection are sure to set your pulses racing and leave you wondering with each turn of the page: are these writers born survivors?

CONTENTS

Callum Bigg (13)	51
Olivia Lindsey (14)	52
Jos Morgans (13)	53
Billy Allen Dighton (14)	54
Lilly Law (12)	55
Teigan Stisi (14)	56
Halima Miah (14)	57
Casey Mai Cripps (11)	58
Holly Fedder (14)	59
Hailie Randall (13)	60
Jude Morgans (11)	61
Beth Oliver (14)	62
Mia Kinghorn (13)	63
Ellie-Mae Young (13)	64
Billy Robbins (13)	65
James Coombes (14)	66
Atish Phembu (11)	67
Nicky Willmott (14)	68
Marion Rudge (14)	69
Lucy-Louise Snelling (11)	70
Luke Saunders (13)	71
Noah Torrance (13)	72
Ava Crawshaw-Thomas (12)	73
Charlie Sharp (11)	74
Joe Jeffrey (13)	75
Joshua Wilson-Hartley (13)	76
Katelin Buckle (12)	77
Luke Scott (11)	78
Hope Lisa Shephard (13)	79
Adam Coleman (13)	80
Aaron Terry (12)	81

The Norton Knatchbull School, Ashford

Jacob Brian Oscar Fisher (14)	82
Samuel Horne (14)	83
Scott Strange (13)	84
Ace Gates (13)	85
William Mendez (13)	86
Mackenzie Drew (13)	87
James Richardson (14)	88
Harry Chapman (14)	89
Daniel Sussams (14)	90

T B (13)	91
Gus Ryan Kay (14)	92
Sebastian Huson (13)	93
Harry Grant (13)	94
Cameron Waller (13)	95
Ben Ward (14)	96
James Pepper (13)	97
James Brooker (14)	98
Robert Mayes (13)	99
Marcus Beare (13)	100

Vinehall School, Mountfield

Milo Morrison (11)	101
Beatrice Mullender (12)	102
Ollie Bearcroft (11)	103
Kawin Watcharotone (12)	104
Daisy Jane Scarlett Fane (10)	105
Izzie Steed	106
Miranda Riley (13)	107
Isabel Troyas	108
Sophie Elizabeth Platt (11)	109
Mia Greenhalgh	110
William Curtis	111
Dmitry Avdeenko	112
Freddie Lawler (12)	113
Clementine Dawson	114
Noah Parkin	115
Chaya Lilly Lynch (10)	116
Fabian E Greenwood (12)	117
Nathan Alexander Lane (11)	118
Lucy Barrett (12)	119
Bertie Maximilian Turner (11)	120
Lucas Maule	121
Ottoline Gee	122
Honor Fox	123
Leo Avery (11)	124
Lara Sassone	125
Billy Mannion (11)	126
Sebastian Declan Pearson (12)	127
Will Steed (12)	128
Mary Keast-Butler	129
Thomas Edward Sturges (12)	130
Ethan Wright	131

THE MINI SAGAS

Last Breath

With one swift blow, there was obliteration. The gritty chippings of the buildings were all that was left of the town, derelict and defoliated. Catastrophe had swept through the metropolis, gushing, flowing, ravaging everything that stood in her way. Devastation foamed, boiling over, clenching the buildings as a last hope. Writhing in her agony, cries radiated out, rubble swept through the land. Shattered and torn, limb by limb, she drained the people how they'd drained her. They had changed her and destroyed her, after all she had given them. For them, nothing was enough. Now Nature took her last breath...

Hannah Bekman (13)
Bromley High School, Bickley

The Beautiful City

The beautiful city destroyed, annihilated. Buildings broken, homes gone. All because of one terrible catastrophe. Grit lay covering the ground. The few people left stood lonely, some crying, some with just a plain expression on their face. All had lost hope. Glass encased the path along with the bodies of those who had died. The mud squelched, but not because it was wet with water but because it was wet with blood. Pillars came crashing down causing a long domino effect across the wide town square. Screams were heard, signalling death. Silence resumed once again in the once beautiful city.

Gabriella Felicity King (12)
Bromley High School, Bickley

We Did Nothing

We have been forgotten. Everyone has been forgotten. Lives lost, hearts broken and homes shattered. Devastation fills us. Now we are lifeless, numb. Catastrophe awaits us again. The days of clear blue skies are gone. The days of poverty, sadness and death have arrived. The polluted air, the broken roads, the sad hills are here. The only thing we have is hope. Hope won't get us anywhere though. What's done is done. There's no going back! Why though? We did nothing. All we did was live. But now we are ruined. We are nothing but ruined, gone and forgotten. Forever.

Ikshula Prasad (11)
Bromley High School, Bickley

World's End

An endless river of fire engulfed the city. A dusty powder from an endless fire bigger than any before rained on what was left of the town. One last scream echoed through the ruins, its pitch deafening, full of pain. In the centre of the catastrophe, causing all this mayhem, lay an enormous dominating volcano which, until recently, was underwater where it couldn't hurt anyone. Now it was the highest volcano in the world and ten times bigger than the mighty Mount Everest. There was a dearth of hope for all countries around the world. The world's end was near.

Shreya Aravinthan (12)
Bromley High School, Bickley

The End

The end was frighteningly near. 2068, the time for World War Three had arrived. Bombs were flying in all directions whilst families ran in fear. Our world was falling apart, nations were fearlessly destroying what was known as Planet Earth with their powerful weapons. A lab in New York had found a way to destroy their opponents with the most autonomous robots that had ever been created. At first, they thought their idea was genius, until they let them run wild. The robots took over and slaughtered women and children without a hint of mercy. The end had come...

Amalia Khatri (11)
Bromley High School, Bickley

Dust

Three seconds. All it took was three seconds! I was far enough away, but my brother and sisters were not so lucky. One, the plane dropped the bomb. Two, it fell so fast that it screamed. Three, all fell silent. I was knocked to the ground, my ears ringing. As I scrambled to stand up, I wondered where everyone went. Then it clicked. They were all around me, covering my clothes, encasing my hair, flying in and out of my lungs! The horrific tragic truth - they had all turned to dust and ash! The day my world was destroyed.

Bethany Sankey (13)
Bromley High School, Bickley

Against The Bolt

Vivid electrical images flashed through my mind like bolts of electricity as I lay on the steel bed of the spacecraft. I'd survived - barely. Vicious vehement electric bolts chased after me like my following shadow. Tears and sweat cascaded down my cheeks as I thought of my family, innocent victims of the treacherous unjust tragedy. I had no time to look back, the most substantial buildings were consumed by blazing blue flames which emitted ebony-black smoke. Running was desultory, there was nowhere to go.
"Ouch!"
A bolt struck my arm. The pain was intense! Now, my time was draining...

Chudaphak Chutiwatwong (14)

Chatham Grammar School For Girls, Chatham

D-Day

Encompassed in her mother's warm vermillion fur, icy bullets of rain attacked the city of trees and leaves. Clueless, groups of birds began retreating with sheer cries of anguish. Oblivious to the chaos in the silence, she picked a banana. It suddenly began to rot. Burnt amber specks spread like a virus over the canary-yellow skin. Branches beckoned their fleeing troops. The emerald carpet crunched as unworldly mammals entered an unfamiliar territory, metal demons slung over their shoulders. *Bang!* The creature's eyes dilated as she touched her mother's still face. A potent rusty smell overpowered the petrichor...

Precious Steve-Popoola (14)
Chatham Grammar School For Girls, Chatham

Waves Of Reality

The startled people of Thailand wander the once bustling shore like lost souls. A strong scent of misery twists through the air as the tragedy sinks into reality. Many are shell-shocked and mentally scarred, including a boy named Arico. Arico lies among the carnage. Flashbacks torture his mind as his eyes sob uncontrollably. All he can remember is the wall of water racing towards the shoreline as swift and unforgiving as an axe, with no emotion or hesitation. Within moments, it had wrapped each victim in its frigid, foamy fingers, taking their lives, like the lives of Arico's parents.

Poppy Ward-Johnson (12)
Chatham Grammar School For Girls, Chatham

A Feral Fire

Smoke travelled through his throat, taunting, tickling him as it danced down. Shrieks, pleading, death was all he recognised around him. No salvation. This, he knew. Everyone knew. The smouldering inferno crackled deafeningly like crunching bones, a reminder of how he would soon sound to the delighted demons of destruction. His one desire was to see tomorrow, yet he was blinded by flames. The traffic light's orange glow isolated him. Because of it, he couldn't drive away. Time ticked. He thought he was gone! But, his name was called. A hand held his. Was he dead or was he saved?

Polly Clifton (14)

Chatham Grammar School For Girls, Chatham

The Whispering Ashes

As the darkness of the fire climbed the trunks of the remaining trees, birds flapped their wings frantically as they dared to escape. Willow ran, nerves rising up inside her as quickly as the acceleration of a cheetah going for its prey. Stopping abruptly, she hopefully looked around to see if the voices she'd heard were there. Silence. The ashes of nature were whispering to her. Scared of her own shadow, Willow reached for her blanket to prevent inhaling too much darkness for her pure innocent soul to handle. In doing so, she provoked a violent tree. *Crash!* Iron curtain.

Lily Page (14)

Chatham Grammar School For Girls, Chatham

Manhattan

Cillian hated this place. Manhattan was loud. The first rumble didn't startle him. The second rumble was louder, more noticeable than the last. Cillian looked around at the passers-by. A few worried faces here and there at most. A third even louder rumble came. *That definitely wasn't a truck.* Then he saw it, a huge wave heading inland, with no sign of stopping! Cillian ran. He ran into a building and sprinted past everyone in his way to reach a higher floor. The tsunami was taller than any building in Manhattan. He wouldn't survive.

Emily Hynes (14)
Chatham Grammar School For Girls, Chatham

Trapped Down Under

The ground began to rumble, the Earth began to shake. A faint scream echoed nearby. Ally paused to hear where it was originating from. She heard the cries of distraught mothers and longed to comfort them. Armed with only a spanner, Ally began to claw her way out of the pool of mud and rocks she found herself in. Her fingernails filled up quickly with dirt, however, she took no notice. Ally dug and searched without stopping, all to no avail. She desperately yearned to hear her mother's loving call for her to wake up, but that call never came.

Victoria Bello (13)
Chatham Grammar School For Girls, Chatham

Tears Of Fire

On a cool night lit only by the orange glow of fire, something terrible was happening. It was going up in flames! Burning! Kirk could not believe that his father's past was becoming his present. It was like the future was hunting him and he didn't want to get caught! Desperately crying, Kirk turned and saw his house crumble to the ground. Fiery warmth filled the air. Kirk embraced the warmth and the hatred in the flame's eyes. It roared with its lion fangs. His dad died in a fire. Why would he have to go through it too?

Lucy Brown (13)
Chatham Grammar School For Girls, Chatham

Blinding Snow

Blinding white fresh powder lies on the ground, supposedly from yesterday's snowfall. Zero risk. 100% fun. Pointing the board down from the peak to the bottom, my trail leads through trees and bizarrely-shaped ice canyons. Right, left, right, over a log, clipping it, nudge it just enough, moves enough to roll, setting all loose snow into motion. Avalanches this month have gone. Ten metres away from the avalanche. The reckoning force is building up. Seven metres. Trees are getting thicker but the force continues. Five metres. The avalanche is near. Two metres. Gathering speed. One metre. Snow, blinding white snow.

Edward Aylward-López (15)
Dover College, Dover

The Rain

"The test, we have it today?" said Stefan. Stefan and Alexis nodded with sorrow. "I wish this damn world would end!" moaned Stefan.
A heavy thunderstorm appeared. The group watched its approach at high speed. Then it started. Outside, people were showered. Their organs disintegrated, vomited out. They convulsed violently. The group rushed towards the school. Stefan was first. He barred the door, only to watch his friends suffer. He knew he must wait for the rain to stop or risk himself. There was a moment of pure silence. The end of the world.

Yzin Khader (14)
Dover College, Dover

The Inevitable Death

A sharp burst of fresh lava bulleted into the sky, disseminating from the volcano like scalding droplets of rain. Deadly clouds of gas enveloped the mouth of the volcano, spreading surreptitiously across the innocent sky like a predator searching for prey. It cascaded down aimlessly towards us. I took the responsibility of vigorously shaking the alarm bell. Italian voices reverberated all over the village as I screamed at the top of my voice to warn them. Children cried, fear flooded the innocent with thoughts of death, inevitable death. Lava approached closer as time ran out...

Kal Mere (15)
Dover College, Dover

A Close Call

The trees swayed and the wind ran. Yellowstone Park was simply unbelievable, well that's what I thought. I saw the ground under my feet start to rumble. I thought, *this is the end of the road.* A sudden blast happened in the distance, blasting molten rock twenty feet into the beautiful sky. My heart was racing and adrenaline took over my body. I left in a flash, but I wasn't fast enough. Cornered, with lava all around me, I said my final prayers and braced myself for the pain. A noise graced my ears. A helicopter appeared! I was safe.

Jaiden Flisher (14)
Dover College, Dover

Dark

It was a usual day, until the clouds darkened to ash-black and lightning as bright as the sun struck. What followed, Jack would never forget.

It had been two years since the virus spread. Jack was alone. He knew it and he hated it. The love his mother had provided had stopped him every time, but not now. Jack got up and left the house, the safe area, and went into the danger zone. The moment he did, he choked. He was strangled, drowning in his blood. He dropped to his knees, dying. He gave in and then, darkness.

Nathan Powell (13)
Dover College, Dover

No More

Ever since the crash, life eliminated. World eradication. Humans turned on each other like savages. I'd compare us to the animals that once roamed the Earth but they cease to exist. We created the one thing that destroyed us. It's always the punch we don't see coming that knocks us down. What we thought was a stable system was so easily decimated. Who would have thought turning a one into a zero would be the end of us? The end of the world. There was no such thing as money. Money makes the world go round. Earth no longer spins.

Clem Maggi Bóo (15)
Dover College, Dover

Eruption!

Climbing up the jagged hacked-out path, Immy stopped at the entrance to the cave. She pulled out her inhaler and took a hard long breath. Taking a sigh of relief, she looked out over the vast emptiness of what she called home. Snatching the wooden ladder from the entrance to the cave, she strolled into the mouth of the volcano. Picking fruits from the trees, she felt the ground rocking. As she dodged the falling rocks, she scurried down the frail ladder. As her left foot reached the ground, a boulder blocked the exit. Her world ended.

Tamzin Amelie Vickers (15)

Dover College, Dover

Alone

Helpless. None of my screams are heard. I am kept awake every single night, plagued by visions of existence rumbling slowly. One by one, loved ones are taken away. When I close my eyes, I see mountains of corpses, none of which I could save. I am a 'lucky' one, one of 100 scattered around the world. We are immune, but are far from lucky. We witnessed the world end, leaving us behind to represent humanity; which will die out with us from the heartbreak of the reality that nothing will save us.

Imogen Langley (15)
Dover College, Dover

Magma Invaders

The volcano finally erupted, its filling spilling. The hot liquid blanketed the land, burning everything that came into contact with it. Everyone evacuated as soon as possible. A couple of hundred didn't make it, their bodies engulfed. The air thickened every second. The black smoke protruded from the sky, filling our lungs with every breath we took. Segments of concrete projected from the flooring. Bubbles burst in the blazing substance. Something swelled up from within the solution...

"Faith, what are they?"

"N-no idea!"

Big Xenomorph-like creatures elevated from the lava, growling at the sight of us, preparing to pounce.

"Run..."

Julia Marcelina Kowal (13)

St John's Catholic Comprehensive School, Gravesend

Running Aground

There was a bang! People were panicking. There was so much damage to the ship that it began to sink quickly. There were about 354 people on board and they all needed to evacuate the ship as soon as possible. They screamed, they panicked and they ran around, not knowing what to do.

"This ship is sinking!"

"We need to leave, now!"

"Is this a dream?" I asked myself.

I realised it was all real! The ship *was* sinking and I froze in terror. I rushed to safety, then I heard another boom. There was fire. The ship was gone.

Kadisha D'Souza (12)
St John's Catholic Comprehensive School, Gravesend

The Flood

There had been a heavy storm. The water had gushed down like beads being sprinkled onto card. We'd been worried as our houses had been filling up with water.

Two days later, gone, all gone. I was floating on a solitary branch that had been ripped from its mother tree. It was horrific. Children and parents were all screaming till their lungs got sore. People who had survived died soon after from dry drowning. Then it was just me. I looked up to the sky and saw God crying because his Earth had been ruined by thoughtless people.

Annabel Heap (11)

St John's Catholic Comprehensive School, Gravesend

The End Of Tehran

It was to be a terrifying day for Iran, not that Mohammed knew it. He was part of a team exploring Tochal Mountain outside Tehran. He was taking time out of the climb to enjoy the view when disaster struck! As he was hanging from a rope halfway up the rock face, the tremors started, building up to a violent earthquake which cracked the rock in front of him. Panicking, Mohammed's hands slipped and he was swinging from his rope, desperately avoiding the falling rocks. The city below crumbled. He wondered who had survived and whether the rope would hold...

Luke McKee (12)
St John's Catholic Comprehensive School, Gravesend

Is It The End?

Kaboom! The noise of the crash was deafening. Silence. Eyes adjusting to the darkness, I saw that the pilot was dead! My seat had broken away from its frame. Undoing my seatbelt, I scrambled for the door. The freezing air hit me hard. I needed help, but high in the Alps, there was no signal. *My bag*, I thought. Grabbing it, I hastily removed my coat, filling it with essentials. Fearing frostbite, I plunged my hands into my pockets. A loud rumbling broke into my thoughts. Snow was cascading at speed towards me. I had to get away, but how?

Milvydas Sadauskas (11)

St John's Catholic Comprehensive School, Gravesend

Tsunami Survivor

It was a cloudy morning. There was a boy named Lieko who was walking slowly on the beach. The sea was grey and muddy. The boy wasn't worried about anything but suddenly, the waves started to become bigger and bigger. He remembered from school that if that happened, there was going to be a tsunami! He started running in panic to the tallest building near the beach. Everybody was in panic and started running towards the top of the building. No one was harmed because the building was strong enough to face the big waves and the old damaged ships!

Luca Baba (12)
St John's Catholic Comprehensive School, Gravesend

The Wrong Costume!

It was the morning of my swimming race and my alarm had not gone off! I was late to catch my train to London. I picked up my bag and ran for the train.

Arriving at the venue, I started to get changed. Oh no! I had picked up my sister's swimming costume instead of my trunks! What could I do? Either miss the race completely or wear my sister's *pink* costume. I headed for the blocks and took off my tracksuit. A roar of laughter erupted from the spectators but I had the best race of my life. First!

Thomas Long (11)

St John's Catholic Comprehensive School, Gravesend

The Inferno

The California wildfires had spread into a small neighbourhood. There was a family of four surrounded by the flames. They had little time to escape! They saw and heard their neighbours screaming and panicking. The fire brigade were on their way, but they didn't arrive in time! The roaring flames deafened the family and the smoke blinded them. Now the only sounds they could hear were the flames and the sirens of the fire brigade. They started to extinguish the flames. But would they all go out?

Eliott Bevan (11)
St John's Catholic Comprehensive School, Gravesend

The Night She Died

"Argh!"

Her scream was deafening. That was the night she died.

Two months ago, we were stolen from our families (who were probably dead now). It was just Hannah and I. We were only known by number. If we spoke our true names, we'd be killed. At the camp, they trained us to fight against our own kind.

"Today is the day we march to war."

We left the camp, hearts in our mouths. We were out. Suddenly, there was a gunshot from behind! I looked around for Hannah.

"Argh!"

Her scream was deafening. That was the night she died.

Jorja Larraine Satchell (14)

The John Wallis CE Academy, Kingsnorth

Avalanche Disaster

The ground rumbled. Snow dropped on my head.
Frightened, I looked back.
"Oh my gosh!" Suddenly, loads of snow was
dripping down the mountain. "Snow, snooww!"
I rushed away from the snow. Lucy screamed
"Avalanche!"
The smoky snow suffocated me, the snow piled
down the mountain. I was darting so fast. Then I
was in a dark place. I was frozen. I couldn't move!
My life was over.
"Why, what, where am I?" I shouted. "Where am I?
Hello, anyone?" I thought I was in a dream, like I
was in a nice sleep. Then trees started to fall.
"Nooo..."

Ruby Watson (11)
The John Wallis CE Academy, Kingsnorth

Run!

The destruction started at eleven. Everyone froze with shock. The 'dormant' beast was raging. The summit splurged out its insides in all directions. Nothing and no one was safe. It crawled through the streets, taking out everything in its path. It was as loud as an incensed lion. The molten rock rippled towards me. I was stuck, frozen in fear.
"C'mon!" Alf shouted. "We need to go, now!"
I was so useless, I couldn't do anything. It slithered closer and closer until it almost stroked my shoes. At the last second, Alf grabbed me, but he wasn't quite quick enough...

Rosie Caldwell (14)

The John Wallis CE Academy, Kingsnorth

The Ending

Gora crawled out of the salty water onto the only land for miles. It was sinking. He thought about what to do. He saw a log. Gora swam. It was almost submerged in the bitter liquid. The remaining land disappeared without a trace. He decided it was better to sink than swim. He dived down into the darkness...

Gora opened his eyes. He was at home with his family! Something tugged at his leg. He tried to scream. Sleep paralysis!

"That flood couldn't happen in real life, it was just a dream, right?"

The world went blue in an instant...

Edith Pearson (11)
The John Wallis CE Academy, Kingsnorth

The Jamaican Hurricane

The Jamaican sky was as grey as concrete. The streets were like a floating village. Thunderous clouds growled. All that kept replaying in my mind was my mum's last words, *"Don't lose hope, Emily."* Ravenous, the hurricane was getting angrier every moment. Swimming through what used to be the market, my grip loosened on my water bottle. My last piece of hope slipped away. I'd lost everything. A gargantuan wave hit me. I was dunked underwater. A gush of coldness trickled down my spine. Every emotion flooded me. Hurt, cold, hopeless. Everything went black. The hurricane had won. Goodbye Earth.

Jemma Louise Allen (12)
The John Wallis CE Academy, Kingsnorth

The Run

Running, running, running. Trying to keep stable as the ground shakes aggressively. Dust fills my lungs as buildings around me collapse. My eyes are getting droopy but I can't stop, I need to keep going. Horror is on everyone's face when the road breaks like it's waiting to devour us. The town will never look or feel the same again. Cheerful families have been ripped apart, beautiful landscapes destroyed, but I need safety. Dodging every broken building piece, I try to find my brother. *He must be here somewhere!* Looking, searching, he is nowhere to be found. *Bam!* Darkness kills...

Katie Bridger (14)
The John Wallis CE Academy, Kingsnorth

The Terrible Wind

I was watching TV with my mum. Everything was fun until I got a notification. It said, 'Tornado approaching'. I ran outside and saw trees coming out of the ground, lamp posts bending and cars lifting! After I'd seen all that, I ran inside and shouted, "Everyone down to the basement, now!" We all got to the basement. I will admit, I cried. I thought I wouldn't live, it was a disaster!
After waiting for like two hours, we came out of the basement. Our house was okay, but I saw trees and cars destroyed and a few houses damaged.

Kiara Cooley (13)

The John Wallis CE Academy, Kingsnorth

Start Of An Odyssey

Ashes cover the once great city, now engulfed in skies of black. Some survivors are in a fragile state. They feed off the remnants of civilisation. Johan speaks, "How do we know we are the last ones left?"

A thought strikes his mind. Johan drinks the last of his water. Then his best friend, Kayno, suggests, "We must move south, there is no point clinging onto a city that shall not provide."

Johan responds, "I agree."

They pack up all they can and start their journey to safer lands. But, there's something lurking in the darkness of the urban landscape...

Ethan Morse (11)
The John Wallis CE Academy, Kingsnorth

Hill-Can Top's Apocalypse

"All survivors, the infected are taking over. Slowly, our population grows smaller. The infected are like rabid dogs, they stop at nothing. Aim for the head and watch your back. Do not go out at night. Travel by day. Use UV lights to keep the infected away. The CDC is trying to find survivors. If you are bitten, it's over. You will turn as quickly as a gun runs out of ammo. You can prevent it. Stay quiet in crowded areas." Screams. "I repeat, stay quiet! If you hear this, head to the CDC now! Survive!" Growls. Screams. Gunfire. Static...

Liam Edward Rumsey (14)
The John Wallis CE Academy, Kingsnorth

Death Upon Us

The land of England is a mountain of rubble. Shattered glass is everywhere.

The shaking of the ground had sent people to the floor and the buildings fell like dominoes. There were only a handful of people who could survive it. The air had felt so cold. I couldn't see anyone or anything, but I could hear everything. People were screaming. I was tugged out of the rubble. They said, "There are only four of us left!"

Now, the food is gone. There's only minimal amounts of water. So, here we are, sitting around a fire with death upon us...

Max Gregory (14)

The John Wallis CE Academy, Kingsnorth

END Project

After World War Three, the world showed its fangs. All of the world's greatest catastrophes began all over the world. The desert had ice storms, Iceland had scorching heat. It was just the start. This was named the END project.

It is now 2056. The world has not let up. People have evolved. People in the desert have become lizard men, people in the sky have become beast men, people on the land have become beast men. The cities are left in ruins with monsters, goblins, giant insects, dragons and mutants. We have all adapted to live here in hell.

Alfie Gardner (13)

The John Wallis CE Academy, Kingsnorth

Toxic Waters

Day by day, the world around me wishes this disaster had never come. Mankind is getting surrounded by the toxic waters that are slowly rising above land, soon to swallow countries whole. Waste is spreading over our lands, poisoning our cities. People are slowly dying. Feet dissolve to ankles and, before you know it, towns and shops have disappeared. Countries will be joining soon, the people gulped up inside. The rancid water is destroying our world as we know it. Cautious with every step I take, our roads are forming bumps under fast rippling waters. Our world will be gone...

Kai Hancock (14)

The John Wallis CE Academy, Kingsnorth

Home?

Waking up, I find my body paralysed under a large rock. In my ears, I can hear people bawling in horror and scattering everywhere like soldiers. The fire is roaring, the water is sinking. Buildings are collapsing with people screaming for help. Smoke and gas is mixing together, creating a toxic scent. Clouds are reaching out to me. There are screams everywhere. For a minute, I don't know where I am. It feels like everything is happening in real life though. Am I dreaming? Has WW3 commenced? Or is this just a nightmare? This place doesn't feel like home anymore...

Riju Limbu (13)

The John Wallis CE Academy, Kingsnorth

The Crumbled Village!

All I remember is waking up to a big shake. I thought it was my little sister waking me up. But it wasn't. The ground shook like a turbo jet. When I looked outside, everything was ruined, everything broken. I remember the smell assaulting me because it was that bad. Now, I'm fed up of sitting in this 'safe' room. We've been here for days, all because the ground has crumbled. I walk up and out. I'm on a hill. As I step outside, the ground beneath me crumbles like a cake. Someone grabs my arm.

"Maddie..."

Jasmin Megan Tiley-Smith (14)
The John Wallis CE Academy, Kingsnorth

Lost

We rose further and further from Earth. I couldn't wait to see the mysterious planets ahead of us. Finally, we reached our destination - space! My excitement only lasted moments before the shuttle split into two. And the only thing holding us up was the zero-gravity atmosphere! People's helmets flew off their heads within seconds, but I held onto mine for dear life. With no oxygen, the team members took their last breaths whilst I was shaking with fear. "How long can I last out here? Where can I get help?" I had nothing, and no one could see me...

Adla Adu-Nsiah (13)
The John Wallis CE Academy, Kingsnorth

Oh My God!

As the volcano erupted, we were thousands of feet away. However, it lit up the sky like fireworks. We were the last survivors. The people near the volcano had tried to build shelters, but I was sure they were dead. It was just me and my family now, the only ones left. All of a sudden, the ground shook. We all spun around. Out of the volcano, came a robotic spaceship with booming speakers. They echoed around the land, "Surrender or die." "Oh my god!" I screamed and I ran.
The sound stopped. I stopped...

Charley Kinggett-Proctor (11)
The John Wallis CE Academy, Kingsnorth

The Invasion

It was once a beautiful town... before they came. I remember it like it was yesterday. Tonnes of them came from space, ready to kill. There were around 100 of us they didn't kill. *Why didn't they kill us?* That question lingered at the back of my head. A couple more ships came to Earth. However, instead of more aliens coming to kill us, they brought futuristic armour. I realised why they hadn't killed us. It was because they wanted us as slaves!

Today was the day I finally escaped and went back home to look at my crumbled town...

Jean Elizabeth Prescott (12)
The John Wallis CE Academy, Kingsnorth

Devastating Heatwave

I no longer recognised the world. Years ago, a scorching heatwave arrived in the immense city. The temperature rose. This happened for years, but it seemed to still be a problem now as it was still getting hotter. My lungs burnt with every breath; it was like breathing fire. Anywhere I went, I couldn't avoid it. It was unbearable. People had been telling me to run, but I refused. I had love for the place! Panic was coming to me. It was the end. The temperature was still rising. We should have listened, we should have advanced somewhere else...

Adam Warren (13)
The John Wallis CE Academy, Kingsnorth

Final Words

I lay there, looking around, watching my life being destroyed. The splashes of death landed around me, taking people out one by one. To my right, a helpless little girl stood, shaking with fear. She let out a cry before running away as fast as her legs would carry her. I then went through a stage of desperation, longing for my family, my friends, my life. But I soon returned to what was awaiting me - a falling building towering over me, about to claim another human. It was then that Death started laughing in victory, celebrating his achievement...

Ellie Barnett (13)

The John Wallis CE Academy, Kingsnorth

Terror Occurs

On a fine evening, I strolled back to my house. I was appalled! It was battered! So was everything around me. I was distraught. All around me were screams and cries of sadness from the torn hearts of the humans in my neighbourhood. With fear rising inside me, I had to run and find somewhere to hide. The ground started to rumble again and everyone feared for their lives. Parts of buildings started to hurtle to the floor. Only a few people found somewhere safe. I was frightened, it was a horrific situation. Finally, the crashes and bangs stopped...

Keyleigh Cooper (14)
The John Wallis CE Academy, Kingsnorth

The Dangerous Wave

It was the weekend and I was going to the shop to get my lunch. There was a massive television playing and I overheard it saying there was a violent tsunami heading towards my town called Little Town! I went and told everybody I could and went back and told my family. I went into my room and I looked outside and what I saw was the most horrifying thing I had ever seen! There were buildings falling to the ground like dust! I screamed, "Mum, Dad! Come here now!"
The wave approached violently. It was close...

Callum Bigg (13)
The John Wallis CE Academy, Kingsnorth

Earthquake

A minute was all it took. In that minute, my entire life, every person on Earth's life, was destroyed. I felt a sudden shudder from the ground that sent chills through my body. Yet that was only the start of it. Men, women and even children started fighting for their lives like wildcats. The Earth had been crushed and crumbled. People's screams pierced the sky, whilst the look of devastation sat on the faces of everyone. I would never be able to forget the sight of a helpless man begging to live. Then clouds of smoke filled my lungs...

Olivia Lindsey (14)
The John Wallis CE Academy, Kingsnorth

A Lone Wolf

When we saw the cloud of flame, we all knew what had happened. Everyone began to rebuild their lives underground. The air outside was parched and everything was out of place. The only things that had survived were some of us and the animals, but they had drastically changed. Sewers had burst due to the blast and the smell assaulted my nose. It was now a kill or be killed situation. People fought for supplies, some even teaming up. Personally, I was a lone wolf, fighting for my own life. The dangerous wasteland was as hard as it could get...

Jos Morgans (13)
The John Wallis CE Academy, Kingsnorth

The Meteor

I was walking to school on a Monday morning and I looked up and saw a big burning ball come plummeting down to Earth and crash right in the middle of my school! I kept going to school because I wanted to investigate what it was or who was behind it.

I finally got to the school door. I crept in slowly and carefully in case there was someone there. I walked down the destroyed hallway. The meteor had done some major damage! I stopped. I heard footsteps. They didn't sound like human footsteps through. They were running towards me...

Billy Allen Dighton (14)
The John Wallis CE Academy, Kingsnorth

Hotter Than The Sun

One mysterious night in London, it was scorching and it was getting worse with every second. There was a beaming light coming closer to the Earth. It was like the sun but even brighter. It was so hot that trees were setting on fire! All of a sudden, the ground shook. People were running whilst trying to keep their balance. Everyone was screaming whilst trying to stay safe. I was lost. I didn't know where to go. It didn't look like home. There were explosions everywhere. There was fire coming from every direction. It was the end.

Lilly Law (12)
The John Wallis CE Academy, Kingsnorth

The World Coming To The End

As I was walking past the shop, I looked in and saw my reflection collapse to the floor. People around me were running everywhere as the solid concrete shattered under their feet. Buildings around me were collapsing and I could taste the dust flying around. Shards of glass were pinging out of the window frames and I could hear the cars flipping over one by one. I could smell fire all around me and I was on my own, helpless, alone with no one around. Darkness grew around me. In my thoughts, there was no hope. My destiny was decided...

Teigan Stisi (14)

The John Wallis CE Academy, Kingsnorth

Shattered

The screams are still playing in my head on repeat. I can't tell if I am alive. I try to open my eyes - still completely black. I try to move - still frozen. The sound of a crying child wakes me up again. I shuffle a bit and realise that I'm underneath rubble. I can smell all the burning of buildings and the sparks of lava settling around me. The shrieks of the child grow louder. I force myself to follow the horrific sound, struggling with fear and there I see a little boy, tears streaming down his broken face, traumatised.

Halima Miah (14)
The John Wallis CE Academy, Kingsnorth

Sail Away

I looked around ready, ready for it. I felt it coming.
Mum shouted, "It's coming!"
We put up the sail and heard the rush of water
coming for us, drowning everything in its way. Then
we saw it - the ocean heading straight towards us!
A cold feeling ran through my body. In less than a
second, all that we could see was the murky water
surrounding us like we were prey. We had no hope.
The waves were like fists trying to punch us over.
Dad said, "We'll be fine," but he looked nervous as
he said it...

Casey Mai Cripps (11)
The John Wallis CE Academy, Kingsnorth

Holiday Nightmare

We finally reached our destination. It had taken over eleven hours. I'd never seen such a crowded airport in my life! I tripped over and all my luggage fell everywhere. Getting into the taxi was so difficult. It was so crowded. When we got to our hotel, I felt like I was the Queen because it looked so beautiful.

The next day, as I went out to the sea, there was a sudden rumble. I froze on my feet as the sea smothered the land. The tsunami wave was huge! All of a sudden, everything went blank...

Holly Fedder (14)

The John Wallis CE Academy, Kingsnorth

Before They Came

All I could hear was my navy heels marching down the corridor. Suddenly, the halls were flooded with screams and the building began to shake! Everybody that ran past me had a horrified look stapled to their face. I heard glass shattering and I noticed people groaning as the building collapsed. I looked around, but I was very calm. I knew what to do. This had happened before. As I stumbled to a desk, I lay beneath it with my arms over my head. Suddenly, everything went quiet. I looked up and saw a green creature staring at me...

Hailie Randall (13)

The John Wallis CE Academy, Kingsnorth

Jungle Fever

We'd done it. The rainforest was growing too much, too fast, too deadly. My team tried to stop it, we failed. It had taken the USA and travelled across water, it was like a tsunami of plants. The news came in... It reached Europe. My group were in the heart of the Amazon with no food as we couldn't eat the food on the trees. We'd seen what happened when a parrot ate some.

We lost someone, I was starting to lose hope. I lost it when the rest of the group disappeared. Something was watching me... It wanted me...

Jude Morgans (11)
The John Wallis CE Academy, Kingsnorth

The Volcano's Wrath

Flames hit me like a bullet. I ran fast, trying to avoid the obstacles ahead of me and charging towards me. Pouring lava chased me while the smell of ash fought with my nose. Smoke stood in my path, but the volcano extended its wrath. It continued to throw whatever it had at me. I was struggling to breathe. Heat battled with my eyes, whilst falling rocks were out to get me. I tried looking for shelter, but the buildings were shattered. I tried searching for a living human, but it was no use. It was like fighting with fire...

Beth Oliver (14)
The John Wallis CE Academy, Kingsnorth

Lurking Lava

Buildings fell instantly to the shaking ground. A horrific sound swept over the town. It began to fill with lava! The town would never ever be the same again. There were the cries of children separated from their parents. The lava was overpowering. It was as hot as the sun. I was in shock, it was like a scene from a horror film! I looked around. The floor was covered, only a patch left to stand in. It went silent. The cries stopped. The lava began to calm. The air was thick. Everything was gone. I'd survived. For now...

Mia Kinghorn (13)
The John Wallis CE Academy, Kingsnorth

Earth's Split

It was a normal day in school. Suddenly, I heard a huge bang. The ground shook and cracked in half! Me and my mates had to jump over the crack, however, some people froze and fell in. I was frightened and exhausted. Everything was either covered in flames or engulfed by water. All I had was a bottle and a group of mates. Everyone said the world would end in 2012, but it was now 2100 and it was finally happening! The water wouldn't stop rushing in and the flames wouldn't die down. Would I survive the horrible event?

Ellie-Mae Young (13)
The John Wallis CE Academy, Kingsnorth

Heartbreak

So it's been six years since it happened and I still can't believe that out of my family, I'm the only one that has survived. I honestly am heartbroken. It was the 11th of September. Well yes, I was in 9/11 but I survived, unlike the other 3,000,000 in New York who didn't. I've been living on rations of food from the bins. Do you know how it feels without any of your family in your life? God took them away from me... Although, God saved me. I have to thank him and I am so happy I'm still breathing.

Billy Robbins (13)
The John Wallis CE Academy, Kingsnorth

Meteorite

I've just woken up. A meteorite hit the Earth. I'm lucky to be alive. I hit my head on concrete. The sound of car alarms is piercing my ears. I can hear nobody and can't see anyone alive. The only people I see are bleeding from their skulls onto the floor, dead. I look to my left. All the windows of Tesco are shattered and completely broken. There is no signal on my phone. I was walking towards Tesco when it hit. I see mysterious aliens walking slowly towards me! I feel dizzy the closer they get. I pass out...

James Coombes (14)
The John Wallis CE Academy, Kingsnorth

Meteor Rush

The meteor shower happened about a week ago. It was devastating, almost wiping out the whole population. Meteors were scattered everywhere. Dents in the Earth were left behind by meteors as big as a house. I was scared, hiding in a factory. I was starving and in pain as the meteors fell. I can still remember it. The news was on when it hit, killing all the crew. I stood in the corner of the factory. I thought it was the end of the Earth. Then, at least twenty big meteors hit the Earth. It was the most devastating hit...

Atish Phembu (11)
The John Wallis CE Academy, Kingsnorth

Nothing

I can still hear the rain and thunder in the distance. I wonder when it will go away. I look around. There is nothing. I scream. The only reply I get back is an echo. I'm sat here thinking how the twister might have swept away my home and family into smithereens. The probability of me finding them is very slim, just like the chance of my own survival. My whole family is gone, potentially. I scream once again, but get no reply. I wish I could go home and not take anything for granted because now, there is nothing...

Nicky Willmott (14)
The John Wallis CE Academy, Kingsnorth

Flood

A minute was all it took. The water had finally arrived, but sadly I was not ready. *Why now?* As my house was destroyed, I saw my home float away. Knowing I could not survive, a roof was the safest place. Climbing, climbing. The wood would not hold my weight. I hurried as it came closer by the second. It creaked and crashed as it came closer. Breathing, breathing faster. I knew I could not stop it no matter what I did. Watching, time was going by. I was holding tightly now to the roof. The water was there...

Marion Rudge (14)

The John Wallis CE Academy, Kingsnorth

The Day I Said Goodbye...

What had the streets of New York become? No buildings left standing, cracks down the whole road, nothing left on the streets. It was empty, empty as the Sahara Desert. Nothing for miles. Half the human race had been wiped out. Nothing like it had ever happened before. No one knew what to do. No one knew who to call. Everyone was lonely in the world. No one to talk to. No one to laugh with. A single cry for help spread through the emptiness. The world spilt and lava started to spew from the ground. Panic rose...

Lucy-Louise Snelling (11)
The John Wallis CE Academy, Kingsnorth

The Wave

It's been fifty years since the tsunami struck. My life hasn't been normal since. That day, I lost everything. All I could see was the ripples from the sea getting bigger and bigger, closer and closer like the sea was about to collapse. I should have run, but there was nothing I could do. The threatening wall of waves became stronger and stronger. All I could think about was my family being stuck or killed by the horrendous tsunami. And there it was, the horrible fantastic wave, streaming towards me...

Luke Saunders (13)
The John Wallis CE Academy, Kingsnorth

The Strike

I climbed the ladder. It felt like I was climbing for ages, but I eventually reached the hatch. I pushed it open. The sky was bright and I squinted as I clambered out of the hatch and onto the ground. As my eyes adjusted, I saw the edge of a cliff in front of me. But there shouldn't have been a cliff there! I approached it, looked over and saw a huge crater that went on for as far as the eye could see. I noticed something moving at the bottom, something that looked like it didn't come from Earth...

Noah Torrance (13)
The John Wallis CE Academy, Kingsnorth

Avalanche!

I look around. A cold chill runs down my spine making me shudder. Around me, the world lies still. I call out for my family. I hear a muffled voice in the distance! I run towards it. I chuck the snow out of my way, revealing my little sister all alone. I clutch her tightly, not daring to let go. I take her down to look for survivors. We trudge through the never-ending snow. We scream when we find our parents deep in the snow; frozen to death. The ground shakes. A new avalanche falls, burying us with it...

Ava Crawshaw-Thomas (12)

The John Wallis CE Academy, Kingsnorth

Salt

It was the 14th of March and there was a tsunami coming. I got horrendously scared at first, but when I calmed down and realised how bad it was, I started to prepare myself. I packed all the supplies I would need, then I heard deafening sirens go off. I thought the news channel had said there would be a couple of days! I started to panic. Suddenly, a strange scent hit me. It was salt. I saw it. The humongous life-threatening wave was right in front of me! Then it hit. Darkness, cold. I knew I was dead.

Charlie Sharp (11)
The John Wallis CE Academy, Kingsnorth

Terrible Tornado

I heard the scream of a child. I looked around. Everything was black. Then I remembered what had happened. I was so terrified and scared that the wind was going to come back. I pushed some concrete out of the way. Then I saw everything. Everyone was gone! The world was as broken as a plate if you dropped it. I turned around. The wind was back, the swirling wind was back! I was petrified. There it was! It came towards me. I started to be pulled back. It pulled me back further. I was screaming...

Joe Jeffrey (13)
The John Wallis CE Academy, Kingsnorth

The Collision

I was on a plane making my way to America from the UK. The moon seemed extremely close to Earth, I could see all around it and it was getting closer and closer. Then suddenly it collided with Earth on America. The gravity was different and it felt a bit lighter. Then a giant wave came towards us, it was still far away, so I hijacked the plane and flew off. The wave nearly caught up with us as gravity was pulling us down. However, I got away and flew back to the UK and secured my family at home.

Joshua Wilson-Hartley (13)
The John Wallis CE Academy, Kingsnorth

The Catastrophe

I was at school. I had English last and was just about to leave, when I heard people screaming and running outside. I went to see what was happening. I heard a lamp post crash onto the concrete. I felt the ground tremble. I ran so fast, I fell over! My knee had been cut open by a piece of glass from a smashed car window. The ground had a crack in the middle of the road. The ground lifted up so high that cars rolled down it! People were dead. I was rolling down the road too. *Bang...*

Katelin Buckle (12)
The John Wallis CE Academy, Kingsnorth

Swim If You Dare

I remember it like it was yesterday, the day that the tsunami hit. Now, we just live in a large Atlantis. Anyone who couldn't swim died days ago. When the tsunami hit, my heart started to tremble with fear. All of the animals are now extinct. The only animals alive are sharks and fish. You have to live like a fish now. When I go to the bottom of the ocean, I see the crumbling houses. When I look at the buildings, I have flashbacks to what happened. I notice I have scales...

Luke Scott (11)
The John Wallis CE Academy, Kingsnorth

Brain Dead

I no longer recognised the world. Where there was once an empty field, there was now a crowd of bloodthirsty zombies! As far as I was aware, there was only me and my mum left. There we were, stuck in a building. I knew, one way or another, we had to get out.

Eventually, the crowd left, so my mum ran through the door and locked it. She began to run to a shop across the road to get us food, but all of a sudden, five zombies surrounded her! Would I ever know if she survived?

Hope Lisa Shephard (13)

The John Wallis CE Academy, Kingsnorth

Zombie Apocalypse

I woke up this morning to the terrifying sound of screaming. I ran to the balcony of my hotel room. The sun was beaming in my eyes. I put my hand up to block the light and saw people running to their cars. But none of the cars started! It was as if someone had let all of the petrol out. Then a strange creature came running out of the hotel. I recognised the creature as soon as I saw it. It was a zombie! I saw more of them running out of the hotel which was now burning...

Adam Coleman (13)
The John Wallis CE Academy, Kingsnorth

Swarm Of Snow

The snow was flooding down the hill. It was all over for me. I could see my fate in the cloud of snow. I couldn't feel my face it was so cold. I did not want to shut my eyes in case I did not open them again. I wanted to huddle up to something, but I could not see anything. I could only think about my family. I did not want to die alone! I wanted to get up and walk home, but I could not feel my feet. I looked up. There was a man there...

Aaron Terry (12)
The John Wallis CE Academy, Kingsnorth

The Crown Versus The Heatwave

"Your Majesty."

Taylor entered the room.

"What is it now, Colonel?"

Taylor answered, "I'm sorry sir, the Meteorological Office have asked for your evacuation as a priority matter."

The king sighed and placed his golden coat over his shoulders.

"What's the emergency?" the king asked.

"They wouldn't be too specific, sir. Something about a deadly heat. They're calling it a heatwave."

In that moment, the most radical series of events doomed The Crown. There was light, then there was darkness. There was silence, then there was noise. There was a scream, a cry, then there was nothing. God save the...

Jacob Brian Oscar Fisher (14)

The Norton Knatchbull School, Ashford

Isolation

The words 'no one will survive' instantaneously gave me a sense of disbelief and impending doom. My primary instinct was to run, run as far away as possible. Yet I knew that wouldn't save me. It would just prolong my inevitable death. Hell had struck and it wasn't going to stop. A sheer massacre of deformed figures littered the desolate wasteland like junk. Dismembered limbs had considerable portions missing. Fires still raged from wrecked vehicles. My contact with humans became increasingly unnecessary. Animals were the only necessity advantageous to my survival. How long I would be there was vastly ambiguous...

Samuel Horne (14)
The Norton Knatchbull School, Ashford

The Extinction Of Humanity

Trees are leafless, plants are dead, people are dehydrated. It's like the world has turned on every human. The streets are filled with beggars, desperate for water, anything to stay alive. The shops are crowded with red-faced people, skin falling onto the floor, throwing up everywhere. Shops are filled with customers covering themselves in sun cream or lying in freezers to cool themselves down. It's the biggest disaster the world has experienced. People don't know what to do, stay in the shade, in a house, in a pool or in the sea. They're just waiting for the heatwave to finish...

Scott Strange (13)
The Norton Knatchbull School, Ashford

Diary

Day three. It's been a few days since the earthquake. I can't remember what life was like before. Civilisation has collapsed and taken everyone with it. I've set up shelter in an office building. There's a radio next to my bed that's happily humming away as if nothing's happened. Day 1,239. I've no idea how long it's been since it happened. No idea when I last drank. My sweet home is crumbling away. I can't leave this building though because every floor below has asbestos! Even Benny the radio is moaning his final tune. I'm about to jump. Goodbye...

Ace Gates (13)

The Norton Knatchbull School, Ashford

Fifteen-Year-Old Versus...

Alone. Mother dead. Father dying. Three metres of water. This was detrimental to the survival of humanity. Florida had seen rain, but nothing compared to this unmitigated flood. Four metres. Water rising, anger rising. Everything I knew floated away. I needed food. I ravenously searched for beans. Five metres. The water was a mammoth crushing me. Even if I could escape, it was like there was a plethora of knives waiting for me. I wanted to float to live, however the debris was surrounding me, wrenching me down. I needed to use a technique no book mentioned - common sense...

William Mendez (13)
The Norton Knatchbull School, Ashford

Volcanic Disaster

I awoke to the smell of hot air which filled my lungs. I gagged, choking on the incoming ash. I turned to the right and saw my wife burning alive! With no hesitation, I rushed downstairs to my dog. I packed food and resources, grabbed the collar and headed for the exit.

Outside, I looked around. There was total destruction! People were melting into the boiling violent lava. It was hell. Crashing and thundering came from close buildings. I saw a body dissolve in the magma. My dog was thirsty. I refreshed him as we travelled further into town...

Mackenzie Drew (13)

The Norton Knatchbull School, Ashford

Heatwave

It's been... I don't know now. Days? Months? Years? I don't remember much. The heat makes you forget things. I've been going down streets I've been down before. There are no longer children playing in the road. Instead, rotting bodies are piled up where houses used to be. The birds and rats that survived the initial devastating impact of the heat now eat away at the maggot-infested decaying flesh. The boils on my skin have started to burst. One of them near my groin is infected. It oozes green pus most days. I don't have much longer left...

James Richardson (14)
The Norton Knatchbull School, Ashford

Dawn Of The Dead

The heatwave was rising. The foul smell of rotting bodies was sickening. Thomas was sitting on his bed, sweat dripping down from his greasy hair. He looked outside, reminding himself of the horror that the heatwave had caused. But something was out of the ordinary. He thought he saw a human moving! No, he must be dreaming. This was the first time in four days, three hours and forty-eight minutes that he'd seen another human! But something wasn't right. His skin was burnt off and one of his eyes was gone. The body turned and stared Thomas in the eye...

Harry Chapman (14)
The Norton Knatchbull School, Ashford

The End Of The Beginning

The heatwave hit. It was horrendous. Children screamed in agony. Men and women bellowed with pain as they were knocked to their knees by the sudden heat. The sensation was numbing, blistering my skin, making it go red and bubble as if it were alive. Crawling on the floor like an insect, a woman holding her baby screamed. Tears streamed down her face as her baby bled out of its mouth, pooling around its mother. Cracks and bangs filled my ears as wood expanded, threatening to collapse. Burning flesh brought me to my knees. Gagging, I crawled on the floor...

Daniel Sussams (14)
The Norton Knatchbull School, Ashford

The Heat

The intense heat suddenly hit me. I doubled over, gasping for air. The sweltering air entered my lungs, charring them. Beginning to feel dizzy, I fumbled around my bag, grappling for water. Hastily, I opened the bottle, pouring the contents over my face. That made it worse. My face bubbled violently. In absolute pain, I dropped to the searing floor. The stench of burning flesh hit me. I attempted to scream, but no sound came out. My hair began to combust. I was a human torch! *So, this is how I die?* I began to feel drowsy. I went blank.

T B (13)
The Norton Knatchbull School, Ashford

Pray For The Prey

We were now the prey. Nature was now the predator. Civilisation was no more. There were just meagre towns dotted around the wasteland. After the volcano had struck, the world had gone into a volcanic winter. Anything within fifty miles of Yellowstone melted away, making it hard to find anything to create a fire out of, but we managed to do it. Although our town was a scrapyard, it was the best we could do. Every day, we prayed for a glimmer of hope, a glimmer of light. Humans were no longer sane, they were more like zombies lumbering around...

Gus Ryan Kay (14)
The Norton Knatchbull School, Ashford

Staying Afloat

The winter was taking its toll on the survivors. The rooftop was caked in snow and the remaining civilians who hadn't moved or died from the stagnant mass of water, stained with blood and excrement from the sewers, were suffering from hypothermia. The stench was the worst part; it smelt of old faeces and only those who had a strong stomach could bear it without gagging. I knew I had to leave or I would surely not survive the harsh winter. But it would be hard to say farewell. If I left at night, I could avoid confrontation...

Sebastian Huson (13)

The Norton Knatchbull School, Ashford

A Man's Limit

The blood has been on my hands for what I can only guess has been eight months. It won't go away. The dead are always with me. Now, they're a part of me. I don't feel ashamed or sad anymore and I am drained of fear. Before, I would have been disgusted with myself for doing what I've done but, out here, it's kill or be killed. I have survived everything: unbearable heat, burning sand and desperate people. It's my turn to rest, finally. I shall take one more life. I will see my family again now...

Harry Grant (13)
The Norton Knatchbull School, Ashford

Last Day In Town

I woke up, my heart still pounding out of my chest, curious to know what would happen next. It was only a few days ago that I'd first had to think to myself, *is this the end?* I still thought that it could be the end for me. It would mean my whole life would go to waste. I would never be able to have some experiences. Everyone was still struggling for food and water. Anything edible we saw, I knew we had to take advantage of. If we didn't, it would be the whole town that would be deceased...

Cameron Waller (13)
The Norton Knatchbull School, Ashford

Going With The Flow

I couldn't understand what was happening. It was getting hotter. I could feel my blood starting to boil. Abruptly, I heard a deafening scream. I quickly ran outside. There was a lady slumped over on the ground, using only a rock to keep herself upright. Her skin was orange and was bubbling, almost as if it was alive. The thick smoke surrounded me. I walked towards the only light I could see. A sudden rush of pain pierced my body and my feet, knees and ankles gave way and brought me to the ground...

Ben Ward (14)

The Norton Knatchbull School, Ashford

Alone

Nowhere to run. One of the biggest avalanches I've ever seen comes down to hit me. Blackout... Where am I? Nothing but snow around me. Dead bodies, frozen. The street I lived on will never be the same. I'm only seventeen. I haven't had a family, I haven't had a job, I haven't had a car, I haven't had a house and I haven't left school. I have so much more to do in my life, I don't want it to end now! When will I be able to see my dear parents? Where do I go now...?

James Pepper (13)
The Norton Knatchbull School, Ashford

Fallout

I looked towards the sky. The sun was glaring into my eyes as I emerged from the shed. The house had been ripped in two. I noticed a body under the rubble. Shards of glass covered the patio. The grass had disappeared. For the first time, the city was silent. There was not even the sound of crickets. But despite this, it smelt normal. I could still smell the petrol from the engines and the odd scent of food. In that moment, I felt so terribly cold and lonely. But then, they lifted the green screen.

James Brooker (14)
The Norton Knatchbull School, Ashford

Swelter

It was three days into the destructive heatwave. My tongue felt like sandpaper, dry and brittle. My skin was now charred. My shoes had lost all comfort. I was down to my last litre of clean water. I had almost run out of food. I decided to go outside. What I saw was horrific. Maggot-infested corpses lay in the street. I was one of the few that had survived. Everyone knew it was better to be alone than together now. Civilisation had fallen. *Most* of the community was now breathless...

Robert Mayes (13)

The Norton Knatchbull School, Ashford

Devastation

I saw it and ran. The lava flowed around me like a pack of vicious hungry animals. It broke everything it hit, pulling down houses and burning the remains. I could feel smoke filling my lungs, stinging my eyes. I could hear it behind me. Quickly, I ran into the open. I was safe now. This was the place I had lived my whole life, it was just burning down in front of me! People were running, panicked and afraid. There was a blanket covering the landscape, hiding the people and the devastation.

Marcus Beare (13)
The Norton Knatchbull School, Ashford

Double Trouble

Whoosh! The waves come in. As I'm walking by the coast, I sense that they're larger than usual. I feel like something is coming, something big, dangerous, threatening. Then I hear rumbles. I feel even more scared. I start to run. I run towards the village. The village of the Arumbayas. *Doosh!*
"The volcano, it's erupting!" I shout to my friend, Leo. I call to him again, but he doesn't hear. Then I look to my left. "A tsunami!" I shout. I am trapped. The lava and water devour me. "Argh..."
And there I am in bed, just a nightmare.

Milo Morrison (11)
Vinehall School, Mountfield

Scarlett's Wildfire

Gasp! I gulped in another mouthful of air, my lungs aflame and burning, my legs and arms stricken with pain from running and my face drawn from the torment I was facing. I heard thudding behind me and turned worriedly to see my brother stumbling after me with the same weariness portrayed on his face.

"Scarlett!" he cried. "Slow down!"

I sighed and slowed to a jog next to his wheezing figure. But then we had to speed ahead, knowing the raging inferno wasn't far behind. It'd taken Mum and we were next in line. We ran like everyone else...

Beatrice Mullender (12)
Vinehall School, Mountfield

Meteor Shower Over London

It could be the next doomsday. The weather forecast reported that there was going to a meteor shower all over the world and its first target was London. After that report, everyone who lived in London went into complete panic. Everyone booked ferries and planes, so there was no way I was going to get out of the city. My friends had the same problem.

Twenty-four hours later. *Crash! Boom!* The meteor shower struck London. Nearly eight buildings were destroyed in the first few seconds.

After many hours of meteor showers, they stopped. London had been destroyed.

Ollie Bearcroft (11)

Vinehall School, Mountfield

World's End

Mike was reading a book when the ground started to shake. It shook more and more every minute, so he ran as fast as he could out of the orphanage. When he got outside, the orphanage suddenly collapsed! He ran to the beach because he thought that it would be safer there. The earthquake was so ruthless that he couldn't stand!

After what seemed like hours, the earthquake finally stopped. The earthquake had wiped out millions of buildings and lives. As Mike looked at the ocean, he saw an enormous tsunami approaching the shore. Could it be the world's end?

Kawin Watcharotone (12)
Vinehall School, Mountfield

Bang!

I would never have thought that my life would come to an end this holiday. I was on holiday with my family in Paris. Our holiday was all going according to plan, until terror struck. I heard a loud bang echo through the air. I looked up and saw big, black, spherical objects falling from the sky. "Mum, what's happening?" I asked, fear rushing through my body.

"I don't know," she replied quietly.

Bombs came plummeting down to the ground. I covered my head with my hands but it was useless. *Bang!* I flew backwards, my heart in my mouth...

Daisy Jane Scarlett Fane (10)
Vinehall School, Mountfield

Peak

Pollution was at its peak but nobody would stop, everyone needed energy, so everyone suffered. The arrow was in the red zone; each day rising a sliver more. First, it was grains of soil and sand, floating outwards into time itself. Then trees, cars and rooftops followed. As the power of gravity weakened, unlucky people were taken, drifting away like balloons on a birthday. The world is getting smaller, space is already limited. Tops of skyscrapers are being decapitated; polar ice caps are no longer submerged. However, we are adapting, we are changing... but only because we must.

Izzie Steed
Vinehall School, Mountfield

Anti-Gravity

Things were getting out of hand. People were floating away into outer space like balloons at someone's birthday. No electricity, no way of contacting anyone, no way of knowing what was being done, no way of knowing *if* anything even was being done. Everyone's life was at risk. They were like lights amongst the stars that could be flicked off immediately by a single switch, never to be resurrected from the blackness of death. What was their fate? Nobody knew. What was their purpose? Nobody knew. Were they ever going to see their loved ones again? Nobody knew...

Miranda Riley (13)
Vinehall School, Mountfield

Wave Of Death

The wave grew bigger and bigger, the shouts became louder and louder, the town was getting smaller and smaller. People were climbing the trees and children were crying pathetically. Mother was trapped in the wheelchair and I could only watch as the big wave forced her into the ground, pinning her down like an animal trapped in its cage.

Why was this happening? Why? *What have I done, God, for you to punish me?*

"If I ever see you, I will kill you," I shouted.

But it's pointless because her death is killing me anyway. My world is dead.

Isabel Troyas
Vinehall School, Mountfield

Dominoes

The ground shook in fury, lifting everything up.
It started off as a distant rumbling; soft and quiet.
The peculiar feeling was like rippling blankets
moving beneath me. I didn't believe it at first but
then I saw it. An earthquake. Instead of screaming,
only a shrill squeak came out. The ground was
moving and buildings were falling like dominoes - I
knew my house would be next...
Frantically, I began sprinting towards the door.
Suddenly, I saw the cause of my death, blocking
my path, luring me in. Cracks were appearing in
the ground. I had to find a way...

Sophie Elizabeth Platt (11)
Vinehall School, Mountfield

Mother Nature's Revenge

Where did we go wrong? Our cities demolished, towns destroyed, nothing left, these monsters are relentless, never stopping, never sleeping, always hungry. Why are they here? As I scour the streets of what remains of London for a morsel to eat, I ask myself if this could be Mother Nature taking her revenge on us for building our concrete cities on top of her once luscious forests and fields? Then I see the unmistakable figure of the tall, black, slimy monster with its razor-sharp teeth! Suddenly, I realise the monster is looking for something to eat - something like me...

Mia Greenhalgh
Vinehall School, Mountfield

Avalanche

Ice, everywhere was frozen and there was nothing to see. I looked around, stillness, there was nothing alive to see so I started to walk home on the frozen wasteland. Then I saw a tank rolling over the endless desert of snow.

"Probably looking for deserters," I said. But I was wrong, it was going too fast. Then I realised.

"Avalanche!" I shouted. This wasn't an ordinary avalanche, this was monstrous. I ran as fast as I could to the tank but I couldn't catch up.

When will the war stop? I don't know. When will the ice melt? Never.

William Curtis
Vinehall School, Mountfield

Vanished

It was months since The Incident happened. We'd started to run out of supplies and for most of us there was no food left, neither heat nor shelter. Because everyone disappears on their thirteenth birthday, there are only little ones left in charge. The plague is sweeping through us, so The Gangs have taken over. The most powerful one of them is Ranolt's gang. They are barbarous, deadly, merciless and vile, and they rule this zone with demoralisation and intimidation.
But my question is: will we vanish one by one on our birthdays, or will we find a solution?

Dmitry Avdeenko
Vinehall School, Mountfield

Ice, Just Ice

Ever since the blizzards raged, nothing's been the same. Many have perished in this never-ending winter. Yet we trudged on still, finding warmth where we could.

Many years ago the snow started falling and nobody could ignore the changes to them and everything else. We found people that were completely covered in hair like yetis. All the animals turned white to match the snowy desert. One by one they all faded away, so now I'm all on my own. Slowly giving in to the cold. Slowly withering away as I'm frozen. Man did this and man is going to pay...

Freddie Lawler (12)
Vinehall School, Mountfield

Crimson Tentacles

It started off as a small candle flame, flickering and guttering in the breeze. The wind blew too hard. The candle was knocked onto the curtain which immediately burst into flames. It licked at the walls, enclosing, engulfing them. It spread across the houses like a plague.

In no time at all, the whole city was ablaze. People were running from a fire beast which would stop at nothing to chase them down.

The crimson tentacles reached out and snatched the innocent. The fire brigade in their red finery came and saved the day. I wish that was what happened...

Clementine Dawson
Vinehall School, Mountfield

Chaos

Charlie woke up, his mother shaking him like a goat ramming him in the chest.

"We've got to go," she cried.

There was a big crash as the window shattered and splintered all over his desk. Charlie looked down at his hands, they were covered in greyish ash. For a few seconds, there was an icy silence. Then chaos. He stared into the night to find that the volcano he was living next to was raging with an orangey glow. The heat from it was like a blacksmith's hot, burning rod. His eyes started to water. *Bang!* Everything went black...

Noah Parkin
Vinehall School, Mountfield

Fire Fighters

A thick blanket of smoke covered the town, preventing light from entering. The flames danced around us like winged tigers and we couldn't do anything, we were trapped in a ring of fire. Some couldn't bear it and took their lives but a few survivors clung to each other. Children were screaming, flames roaring, souls were sacrificed mercilessly. Looking around, I saw a young girl clinging to her mother. Even though we were both in the same situation I thought that she was lucky, she was lucky because she still had a mother. The flames had already taken mine.

Chaya Lilly Lynch (10)
Vinehall School, Mountfield

Volcanic Destruction

The streets are full of ash, buildings burnt to the ground, water turned to rock, people are shrouded. I smell burning in the air, there's black smoke emerging out of the volcano and lava scorching down the mountain destroying everything in its path. There are chilling screams in the distance which never seem to fade.

My parents have been taken by this destructive beast and turned into ash figures lying motionless in the setting sun.

Maybe one day they will be freed from their ashy prisons. As I walk away I feel they are trying to speak to me.

Fabian E Greenwood (12)

Vinehall School, Mountfield

Blood, Fire And Water

A tremor; a sound wave of destruction; a cloud of ash rushing towards us... I was in Milan - miles from the heart of the action. But we couldn't mistake it. Within seconds, Big Boy came barging through the door; an explosion designed for catastrophe, the extermination of the human race, the end of the world as we knew it. Everyone could foresee what was coming: a tsunami higher and deadlier than any before. What was that man with the gloved finger really feeling; fear, regret or unearthly hatred?

I felt the wave reaching out to me. I held my breath...

Nathan Alexander Lane (11)
Vinehall School, Mountfield

Powerless

I was on a mission: to divert all of the world's power to this box in Hokkaido, Japan. This moment in 2225 was the start of Earth's energy efficiency programme. I just needed to flick a switch. I reached an icy hand out and flicked the switch. If anything went wrong, the world would have no electricity forever! That was when I heard it, a rumbling echoing from a mountain. The snow was cascading towards me, towards the power! It reached the box and, with that, the electric whir of the machine stopped. The world's electricity had gone dead forever.

Lucy Barrett (12)
Vinehall School, Mountfield

Death Wave

I ran to port side and leaned against the ferry rail desperate to see where everyone was pointing. In the distance, I saw a wall of water surging towards us, destroying everything in its path. Everyone was screaming with fear and scrambling to get off the boat. I noticed an abandoned little girl in a panic as the wave defeated the Statue of Liberty. Grabbing the girl, I sprinted to the lifeboat, already lowered into the angry water. Suddenly, the wave threw me overboard, dragging me down to the depths. This was the end. I was face-to-face with death.

Bertie Maximilian Turner (11)
Vinehall School, Mountfield

Hot Flood

It was a flood. Not only a flood, but a burning flood. It had been going on for months. There was nowhere to go. All of the hospitals and rescue stations were flooded so people were staying wherever they could. You could find them on rafts made of mattresses and on boats, their skin bubbling.

"Matt, is that you?"

"Yes," I said.

He slowly started walking away from me.

"What's the problem?" I asked.

He didn't reply. After seconds of silence, he answered, "Your eyes are... burning!"

Lucas Maule
Vinehall School, Mountfield

What Have We Done?

A loud rumble, the ground started shaking so violently I almost vomited. I was petrified. I opened my mouth to scream but nothing came out. We had never had an earthquake in England; it could have been something to do with the climate. I dashed desperately under a car for cover. The ground shook again, throwing the car off its wheels and leaving me with no protection. I screamed louder, hoping to catch someone's attention. Suddenly, I felt a violent tug at my arm; a man pulled me off the crumbling road and called, "What have we done?"

Ottoline Gee
Vinehall School, Mountfield

Defeated

I crawled out of the shelter gingerly and surveyed the obliterated landscape in despair. It was as if time was standing still. The London Eye had crumbled into the Thames. The Shard had disintegrated into smithereens on the previously quaking and tremoring ground. Tower Bridge lay defeated in the river, its once strong rivets and iron cables were twisted and bent as if they were elastic. I glanced up at the sky. A thick cloud of smoke, probably from the volcano which had caused the earthquake, was rapidly approaching London. Could this be the end?

Honor Fox
Vinehall School, Mountfield

Mission Catastrophe

Milo woke up and looked out the window. People were rushing around with scarves covering their faces. An outbreak of poisonous plants had wiped out almost the entire human race! He wrapped his scarf around his face and ran outside. People were running like headless chickens, trying to find shelter from the plants. Milo let people into his house to take shelter and he tried to kill all the plants. But, as he was cutting one of the plant stems, he breathed too heavily and inhaled some of the poisonous gas! Milo gasped and everything went black...

Leo Avery (11)
Vinehall School, Mountfield

Disruption, Destruction

Tonight will be the night they'll regret... our group will destroy their evening. After we have bombarded them, there will be disruption all over town. Hundreds of people will vanish before me. My gunshots will scare the living daylights out of them. The city will be red, red as their blood. The trains will be jam-packed, I will target them too. There'll be screams from the people sounding like horns from a car. Everywhere will be mayhem and all by our hands. This will be the last thing I write because my group and I just want to die...

Lara Sassone
Vinehall School, Mountfield

Disaster

Boris and Jenny woke up to see water flowing up their ankles towards their knees. The tsunami had made its way towards the desolate warehouse in the forest and was seeping through a crack in the wall. Boris went to open the door, but the water outside blocked it. He then tried to kick it down while Jenny searched for another way out. But there wasn't one. As the water rose up, now to their waists, Jenny started to help Boris, but eventually they gave up hope. Then the water covered their mouths as they took their last terrifying breaths...

Billy Mannion (11)
Vinehall School, Mountfield

Survival

The animals had taken over. Everyone was clinging onto something high up so the creatures wouldn't get the chance to rip us to shreds. The animals had made the town hall, the church and even the supermarkets their own.

I was grasping onto an electrical pole that was wedged between two branches. It was getting close to twilight and this was when everyone thought that the animals were going to take their chance to do whatever they wanted to do with us because within hours the majority of us would fall asleep. Then it happened...

Sebastian Declan Pearson (12)
Vinehall School, Mountfield

Back To Life

The ground started to rumble uncontrollably. Felix turned around to see the so-called 'dead' volcano coming back to life. Panic swept through his body. He was hiking up the mountain and had just hooked himself onto it. He knew he had to get himself off the cliff face or he would be a sitting duck. Without warning, a massive cloud of smoke plummeted down the cliff! It was soon apparent that the cliff was acting as a massive shield. Just as he thought he might be safe, a stream of lava poured down next to him, scalding his arm...

Will Steed (12)

Vinehall School, Mountfield

Hospital Takeover

A virus, a lethal virus, is spreading round like the plague. Just like the others, I am one of the many casualties in line waiting, waiting for help. The virus is burning us from the inside out; decaying our bodies minute after minute, another limb turning black and decaying into dust. The virus is taking over the population of America and soon it will be the world. There is no escape, no cure. It is stopping life's circulation; it is stopping the human race. Nobody knows what to do, But we know our end, and we know it is coming.

Mary Keast-Butler
Vinehall School, Mountfield

Nothingness

The tsunami hit before we could run; before we could prepare. I was the only one still standing for miles and miles around. Everyone and everything was gone. My mouth exploded with fury and frustration as I fell onto my knees. I closed my eyes, hoping when I opened them I would see my family standing next to me, but no. I looked up. *There's... there's another one.* I ran and ran for my life, until I realised that there was no point. I stopped, fell to the ground and lay there silently; as the water flushed me away...

Thomas Edward Sturges (12)
Vinehall School, Mountfield

England Under The Sea

A tsunami has just hit a small town in the south-east of England. It's massive, it will cause mass destruction and it's heading for London. I can see it coming. Children are screaming and I can hear a helicopter passing. This is a disaster; I'm waiting for the flood to reach me. It will certainly rise above me. This is the end of me. I get swept away. The flood is carrying me at high speed and will reach London soon.

People are going wild. I grab onto a tree and my neighbour gets swept away, screaming for help...

Ethan Wright
Vinehall School, Mountfield

The Bite Of Death

I remember running, my sister clinging to my back. It wasn't just us; everyone was panicking or rushing around. While others were lying on the cold, hard road clutching their necks with relatives weeping by their side. After running for a while we met a swarm of black moths. I told my sister to stay behind me. I suddenly remembered the gas masks we made in history. I could get them and they would cover our necks. But it was too late. I turned around to my little sister in a heap on the floor, hands fastened around her neck!

Francesca Freedman
Vinehall School, Mountfield

Darkness

Bang! There was a massive eruption and scalding lava came rushing towards me. I sprinted as fast as I could to the junkyard where I had made a boat out of a stash of obsidian I'd found the previous day. All I had to do was hope, hope that my boat would survive the lava.

When it finally came, the boat worked and I was sailing around. At that moment, I heard a small scream for help. I sailed towards it but strangely, I was getting lower and lower until I was swirling round and round and darkness closed in...

Margot Fernau (11)

Vinehall School, Mountfield

Lava Rising

After the explosion of the volcano in Italy, everyone was afraid. Lava was filling the lakes, ponds and even seas. Jake's parents had died after the blast of lava and ash rained down onto their house. Jake built an unstable house at the top of a mountain as the lava started to rise. He was starting to run out of food, so he'd soon have to search for some. He grabbed his machete and ran down the hill towards an orange tree. He cut the branches off and started to run back up. The lava pursued him. He was trapped...

Samuel Rummery (12)
Vinehall School, Mountfield

Sea Dog

The sea dog scampered towards me like an excited puppy, snatching buildings up in his strong jaw, tearing them to bits, only to throw them down on the ground and kick them away at the sight of a new, more exciting chew toy. I looked around at the chaos the giant animal caused; people were running and pushing each other, starting cars and hiding children. Havoc!

I stared at the black pit of water rushing towards me and knew that it was the end. The giant sea dog rushed over me and left me in a sea of black bubbles.

Matilda Godfrey (10)
Vinehall School, Mountfield

The Great Fire

Jake woke up and swore loudly enough to wake up Freddy. Last night, they had got miles away from the fire, even putting rivers between them and the fire. But now, the fire was only metres away.

In minutes, they were on their quad bikes speeding away. The fire was now moving very fast and had dominated most of the forest and the gap to get out was closing. A deer shot past and then stopped dead and looked around, agitated. It was then that Jake and Freddy realised that there was only one dangerous route out...

James Wills (11)
Vinehall School, Mountfield

Frozen

Ice everywhere! It's all you can see for miles. We all thought this day would never come. There are only a few of us left. If we had known earlier, there would still be thousands of us. The ice has destroyed our whole world. I stand at the top of Everest, the only safe place left. When I breathe, it looks like I'm smoking. Each breath I take is more painful than the last. This can't go on for much longer, soon the human race will be no more! We should have listened to them from the very beginning...

Isabella Mia Freedman (13)
Vinehall School, Mountfield

Fading Away

A gush of air sprinted through the beautiful city of Los Angeles. I knew something was up, something, I didn't know what, but it was something and it was waiting, waiting to pounce. Suddenly the water broke into a rush; snatching the palm trees and destroying everything in its path. It picked up buildings as if they were paper and dropped them like they were feathers. Time stood still as the water froze, covering the city like a blanket. All you could hear was the last toot of the birds softly fading away.

Olivia Selmon (11)
Vinehall School, Mountfield

The Earthquake To End All Earthquakes

"Get up!" said Tom. "We don't have much time." He was right, the earth was crumbling and falling down. No one knew why, but whatever the case, Tom and Amy, his twin sister, had to get back to the research station. Their helicopter was there and if they did not get back to the station, they would not get back in time to save themselves. The ground was breaking up as they sprinted across the Arabian Desert. They were not going to make it... Or were they?

Joe Payne (12)
Vinehall School, Mountfield

Trust Nobody

All was silent. Fear sprinted along my spine. I couldn't move. I had a gun that I'd found on the floor covered with blood. I could hear the bullet clip shaking in time with my hand. The virus had covered the whole city; only a few people had survived it. I finally scraped together enough courage to move. If I stayed there, I would eventually be found. I stood up. My boots trod on the broken glass that crunched under my feet. Suddenly, I heard a shriek in the distance. I knew the end was near...

Ludo Green (13)
Vinehall School, Mountfield

Madness

As I woke up I felt a sharp pain in my head and my hands were covered in blood. I stood up and looked around. It was complete madness. I could hear children screaming for their mothers and men with balaclavas were smashing all the windows and taking everything, like children in a sweet shop. I could taste grit on my tongue and my head felt like thousands of blunt nails were being hammered into my head. Suddenly all I saw was darkness and I knew it was the end for me.

Oliver Levy
Vinehall School, Mountfield

Crisis Averted

I was walking back from my kung fu class when suddenly, something caught my eye. It was a tiger eating the zookeeper, shredding his flesh! It looked as though all the animals had started doing the same thing all around Beijing, as though they had something in their minds which was making them crazy! When I got on my way in my car, I saw a lion, so I got out and used my tai chi to make all the animals go back to their ordinary selves. Everything was peaceful.

Basil Sturdee (11)
Vinehall School, Mountfield

Nico The Survivor

Meteorites were falling everywhere and Nico knew that he could not fend them all off. So he ran out of his tractor, just before it blew up! Luckily, he had only been slightly bruised. He removed a piece of burning debris, ran to his old Mustang, slammed his foot straight down on the metal and zoomed out of the area, only stopping for a chocolate cookie because he was feeling a tiny bit peckish. After that, he moved to England and lived happily ever after.

Boudewijn Piet-Hein Mark Chinedu Igbokwe (11)
Vinehall School, Mountfield

It All Came To An End

My life was in someone else's hand. This was the end, the end of me, the end of all those moments, the end of my adventure, the complete end; I wish I could have done more, but once again I'm too late. All I could hear was a little voice whispering in my ear saying, "I will miss you, but everyone has to go to sleep sometime."
It was tragic, sad and painful saying goodbye but as that voice had told me, my death had come.

Isabel De La Lastra
Vinehall School, Mountfield

YOUNG WRITERS INFORMATION

We hope you have enjoyed reading this book – and that you will continue to in the coming years.

If you're a young writer who enjoys reading and creative writing, or the parent of an enthusiastic poet or story writer, do visit our website **www.youngwriters.co.uk**. Here you will find free competitions, workshops and games, as well as recommended reads, a poetry glossary and our blog.

If you would like to order further copies of this book, or any of our other titles, then please give us a call or order via your online account.

Young Writers
Remus House
Coltsfoot Drive
Peterborough
PE2 9BF
(01733) 890066 / 898110
info@youngwriters.co.uk

Join in the conversation!

 YoungWritersUK    @YoungWritersCW